A MASQUE FOR THE QUEEN

Antelope Books

The Dutch are Coming
The Runaway Serf
GEOFFREY TREASE

Goldie
The Time Button
IRMA CHILTON

Dragons Come Home!
The Youngest Kite
JANET MCNEILL

Saturday Shillings
The Seagull
PENELOPE FARMER

The Amazing Mr. Prothero
HONOR ARUNDEL

The Holiday
Peter and the Jumbie
A Bit of Magic
DOROTHY CLEWES

The Chief's Daughter
A Circlet of Oak Leaves
ROSEMARY SUTCLIFF

The Reindeer Slippers
BARBARA WILLARD

This Summer, Last Summer
The Humbugs
MARY TREADGOLD

and many other titles

A MASQUE FOR THE QUEEN

GEOFFREY TREASE

Illustrated by KRYSTYNA TURSKA

HAMISH HAMILTON

First published in Great Britain 1970
by Hamish Hamilton Children's Books Ltd.
90 Great Russell Street, London, W.C.1
SBN 241 01872 2

© *1970 Geoffrey Trease*

Illustrations © *1970 Krystyna Turska*

For Diana Burgess

Printed in Great Britain by
Ebenezer Baylis & Son Limited
The Trinity Press, Worcester, and London

AUTHOR'S NOTE

Queen Elizabeth the First lived from 1533 to 1603 and ruled England for forty-five years. This was a famous period in history. It was the time of William Shakespeare, Sir Walter Ralegh, Sir Francis Drake, and many other people who are still remembered.

It was a dangerous time and the Queen had enemies. There was King Philip of Spain. He had been married to Elizabeth's half-sister, Mary, who had been Queen of England herself until she died. Philip said that Elizabeth had no right to the crown. Once he sent his fleet and army to invade England — the Spanish Armada — but Elizabeth's navy stopped them, helped by the bad weather.

There were plots to murder Elizabeth. Most of her subjects were loyal to her and loved her, but a few joined in the plots. And just after her death the next ruler, King James the First, nearly *was* blown up with all his Parliament in the Gunpowder Plot of 1605.

This story is fiction, but it is close to the facts of the time. England is still full of great houses like "Fairfield Hall" that were newly built in Elizabeth's reign. She did tour round the country—it was called "going on progress"—and the letter which excited the Morland family so much is very like a real one sent to Sir Francis Willoughby in 1575. The musicians' pit, the Hungarian horses with their orange tails and manes, the way the Yeomen of the Guard made the Queen's bed and tasted her dinner, even the names of the dances—all these details are genuine.

CHAPTER ONE

"A FINE THING!" cried Father as he laid down the letter.

"A fine thing," murmured Mother. But her tone was so different from Father's that the children looked from one parent to the other with puzzled faces.

"A great honour for the family," said Father, throwing up his head proudly so that his neat red beard jutted like the prow of a ship.

"Of course, my dear. And a great upset for the household! And the expense will ruin us."

"Nonsense, Kate! We shall manage—"

"Read Sir John's letter again. You know the part I mean."

Nick and Celia waited eagerly while Father held up the letter, scanned the

spidery handwriting, and read the words aloud like a herald's proclamation:

"*Her Majesty has decided to stay two nights at your house. You have need to consider how your supplies of food and drink may hold out. You must take thought also whether you have enough servants, you can scarce do with less than fifty people in attendance—*"

"You see," interrupted Mother in a stricken tone.

Father only laughed at her fears—as he always did.

"We have more than forty as it is. We can engage more. A hundred if you like. Spare no expense."

"You do not realize, Henry! When the Queen travels with her Court, it is like a small army!"

But Father seized her gaily and took her jigging down the long gallery as fast as his lame leg would allow him. The children rushed after them, laughing, and caught up as Father stopped and cried breathlessly:

"I have faced an army of Spaniards— the Queen's enemies. Shall I be frightened by an army of her friends?"

"Oh, it's *wonderful* news, Mother," said Celia, venturing at last to break into her parents' conversation.

"Of course it is, poppet," Father agreed.

And, big though she now was, he clapped his strong hands upon her waist and swung her up to the length of his arms, bellowing with delight. "Of all the houses in the neighbourhood the Queen has picked ours. Are we to say 'no'? Shall we answer, 'Sir Henry Morland cannot afford bite and sup for his sovereign? Lady Morland is in too much of a tizzy about clean sheets and candles?' Shall I write back to Sir John and say—"

"Don't be foolish, my dear," said Mother. "You know you cannot. You cannot refuse Her Majesty. I agree, it is a great honour for us—if all goes well, it may do you much good in the Queen's eyes. But you must understand it is all so sudden—it is a great responsibility, and it all falls upon the lady of the house. I shall have a thousand and one domestic things to arrange, while *you* have nothing to think of but making your bow and paying the Queen a few compliments—"

"Nothing? *Nothing*?"

Father's smile faded. He looked hurt, and for a few moments his eyes were as anxious as Mother's. His tone was grave as he went on gently:

"I shall have my own cares. While the Queen stays under our roof, it is for me to make sure that no danger threatens her."

"Danger, Father?"

This time it was Nick who exclaimed.

Father looked down and nodded. "The Queen has enemies."

"But not *here*?" Celia protested. "Not at Fairfield."

"Not among our own people," said Father. He hesitated. "But there are others. The King of Spain has his secret agents, and there are Englishmen too who hate the Queen and would take any chance to—"

"To kill her?" said Nick.

Again Father nodded.

"Oh, *no!*" said Celia. The joyful excitement had gone from her face. Father leaned forward and pinched her cheek, his own good humour returning.

"Don't be afraid, poppet. Nothing terrible can happen in this house. We shall take care of that. In any case, the Queen will bring plenty of good strong men of her own to guard her."

"And they will all have to be fed," said Mother. "We shall need mountains of beef and oceans of ale. And we have only ten days before Her Majesty arrives."

"Time enough," said Father.

"Spoken like a man," said Mother. "For a woman there is never time enough." But she was smiling again now. She was a good manager, and once she had recovered from the shock of the news, she was ready to cope with all that was needed.

Nick and Celia were bubbling with questions to ask, but before they could ask them their elder brother and sister came into the gallery and the great news had to be told all over again.

"Wonderful!" cried Margaret, and swung round to face her mother. "What shall we wear?"

"Does that matter?" said Father, teasing her.

"But of course, Father!" Margaret's grey eyes flashed like dagger-points. "The Queen is not just coming to eat and sleep— not for two days and nights. She will have to be entertained—"

"You think so?"

"*Father*! We must have dancing here in the long gallery—or would the banquet-hall be better? You know the Queen loves dancing—"

"I know my daughter does."

"The Queen loves riding too," broke in Edward. "Father, could we take her stag-hunting in the park? And get up a tournament for her to watch in the court-

yard—ask all the young men in the neighbourhood—"

"Oh, *yes!*" screamed Margaret.

"You are not always so keen on your
brother's ideas," said Father, his own eyes
twinkling with fun.

"Oh, a tournament in the day-time
would be splendid. The dancing is better
when the candles are lit—"

"You mean you fancy your own looks
better by candle-light," said Edward. He
liked to copy his father in teasing his
sisters and brother.

Edward and Margaret babbled on about
tournaments and dances, the young friends
and neighbours who must be invited, and
the fine new clothes they would have to
have.

Nicholas looked at Celia and Celia
looked at Nicholas. The girl's lips moved
silently, framing the words: *What about us?*
But the chatter of their elders swept along
over their heads as though they did not exist.

Nick liked the idea of the tournament, though he was much too small to take part himself. Celia would not even enjoy watching. She would be too nervous lest the horses were hurt as the young men charged at each other with their lances.

Both children feared that they would be packed off to bed by the time the dancing was under way.

It was as though Father read their thoughts. His deep voice cut suddenly across the argument between his elder son and daughter.

"We'll have all that," he promised them, "and more besides. We'll get up a masque to entertain the Queen—"

"A masque!" Margaret clapped her hands. "Yes, Father. That would be wonderful."

"What's a masque?" Celia hissed in Nick's ear.

"Sort of play," he whispered back.

"Only more music, and gorgeous clothes —not so many speeches—"

Their elder sister had everything planned in a moment. "I shall dress up as a goddess," she announced, "and Edward can be St. George in silver armour."

"I think not," said Father quietly.

"Not? But why not?"

Margaret did not look quite so pretty with her mouth gaping open in amazement.

"You and Edward will have quite enough to do, galloping about after stags and everything else. You would not want to be too tired to dance in the evening." He chuckled slyly. "No, the masque shall be acted by the young folk. Mr. Tuggy shall write it for us. And I shall tell him to give good parts to Nicholas and Celia."

CHAPTER TWO

MR. TUGGY was the master of the
grammar school in the town nearby.
Edward said he was not a good schoolmaster because he was gentle and kind and
hated birching the boys who had not
learned their lessons.

Nick, who attended the school, liked
Mr. Tuggy for that very same reason.

Certainly Mr. Tuggy seemed as pleased
as the pupils when he was told that there
would be no more ordinary lessons until
after Her Majesty's visit. The local children
would be far too busy getting ready to
entertain her.

Mr. Tuggy himself would be busier
than any of them. He had to write the
masque and rehearse the performers. Besides that, he had to compose a long speech

of welcome in Latin and recite it to the
Queen when she arrived.

"Everything must be right, everything
must be ready," he kept saying as he

fussed over the programme and the pre-parations.

Behind his back some of the village boys made fun of him, imitating the way he trotted round with quick nervous steps and the squeaky voice in which he cried: "Everything must be right, everything must be ready."

It became a joke with the children. "Right and ready?" they asked each other with broad grins. "Right and ready!" came the shout back.

Luckily it had been a fine dry summer and the signs were that the weather would hold well into September, so that the masque could be acted in the open air.

Mr. Tuggy called the first rehearsal at the spot he had chosen, a stretch of grass beside the lake, not far from the boat-house.

"The boathouse," he said, "can be our tiring room."

"What's a 'tiring room'?" Celia whispered to Nick.

"Where we change into our costumes," he told her. "Our *attire*."

"Of course! I see."

Father had built Fairfield Hall when they were babies—Nick could just remember moving into their fine new home but Celia had been too young.

The great house stood on the top of the low ridge overlooking the lake. It was of warm red-brown stone, with clusters of chimneys like organ-pipes and little turrets the shape of pepper-pots wherever there was a corner to place one. It was a light, cheerful house with so many big windows that when the sun flashed on them it shone like a huge lantern.

The lake was artificial. Hundreds of men had dug out the earth, dozens of farm-carts had carried it away to another part of the deer-park, and a stream had been dammed to provide the water.

Now the lake looked as though it had been there for ever, a smooth expanse of blue, pricked with green reeds round the edges and backed with woodlands on the far side.

It was a perfect setting for the masque, if only the weather kept fine.

There was a flat area at the water's edge that would be ideal for acting and dancing if the grass was scythed short. Clumps of bushes to right and left would screen the players while they waited for their cues to enter. There was a gentle slope facing the lake. Most of the audience could sit there on cushions or on cloaks spread out. For the more important guests the servants would take down stools and benches.

For the Queen herself, Father said, a special little pavilion must be built. It would be a wooden platform, well raised above the ground so that Her Majesty should get a clear view of the performance and would not catch cold if the earth was damp. Crimson hangings would keep off any chilly breezes and a golden canopy would shield her from an unexpected shower.

"Everything shall be right," Mr. Tuggy promised Father. "Send the workmen in good time, that is all I ask, Sir Henry. Then we shall be ready on the day."

Everyone was hard at work from morning till night—and often long afterwards. The house had to be made ready for the guests, the bedchambers swept and perfumed, the kitchen and larder and dairy and wine-cellar stocked, the stables prepared, cartloads of fodder brought in, and the courtyard set out with barriers and palisades for the tournament.

No one worked harder than Mr. Tuggy. He sat up far into the night composing his Latin speech and the verses for the masque. Most of the children's parts he copied out himself.

He came to rehearsal bleary-eyed with

lack of sleep, his pale hair sticking out from under his cap like wisps of damp hay. He looked happy, thought Celia—much happier than she had ever seen him coming from the schoolhouse after a long day's teaching.

"Mr. Tuggy is a poet at heart," she had overheard Mother say, "he is not strict enough for a schoolmaster."

Celia understood why Mr. Tuggy seemed happy now. He might fuss and chivvy the children when they did not know their lines or spoke them wrongly, but he was doing what he liked and the children were doing what *they* liked.

"And what is the masque about?" Edward asked one day at dinner.

"It's a secret," said Nick, and gave Celia a warning scowl to keep silent.

"Mr. Tuggy does not want the children to talk about it," said Mother quickly. "The audience will enjoy it much more if they do not know what is going to happen next."

Edward looked sulky but dared not ask more.

In fact, thought Nick to himself, even if Edward had twisted his arm, he could not have told him clearly what the masque was about.

It was all so grown-up and Mr. Tuggy had made it so learned. There was no very clear story—the main thing about a masque was to make a stately show, with music and superb costumes and surprise effects.

The performers had to dance, or skip about, or walk in procession as Mr. Tuggy trained them. As for the lines, they must recite them clearly, looking towards the Queen's pavilion, and if they did not understand every word this somehow did not seem to matter.

Some of the characters were Greek gods and goddesses that Nick had heard about at school. Celia was Diana, the goddess of the Moon and of hunting—she looked right for a Moon goddess, for her hair was palest gold in colour and had a fine sheen when it was properly brushed. She had to enter carrying a silver bow, but at the first rehearsal she had nothing but a branch to hold, and the paper with her words written on it. Knitting her brows over Mr. Tuggy's handwriting she recited doubtfully:

"Well met, Apple-oh, Lord of the Golden Day—"

A roar of laughter from Nick and the other boys drowned the next words.

"Not Apple-oh," said Mr. Tuggy

gently. "A-poll-o. You know, my dear—
Apollo, the Sun God."

Celia's cheeks flamed, and she looked
more like a red sunset herself than the
moon she was supposed to be. But soon
she forgot the boys' laughter and began to
enjoy herself. Mr. Tuggy said she was
shaping very well.

Nick played the part of Apollo. That
was suitable because Apollo was Diana's
brother. Nick and Celia had a strong
family likeness but Nick's hair was curly
and he had inherited his father's reddish-
gold colouring. With the sun behind him
he seemed to wear a fiery halo.

The two young Morlands had the best
parts. There was only one thing Nick was
sorry about. He envied the boys who were
Evil Spirits of the Forest, because they
were going to wear ghostly masks with
horns and had to rush in, capering and
yelling, and letting off fireworks to startle
the audience.

Still, one couldn't do everything. It was really more splendid to come in again as Apollo with a magic wand, and scatter all the Evil Spirits, and then end the masque by walking forward to the Queen's pavilion, bowing low, and making a loyal speech. For, as Mr. Tuggy explained, the Evil Spirits really stood for the Queen's enemies, and Her Majesty would understand that, and be pleased with Apollo and Diana for driving them away.

"It will have a powerful effect," said Mr. Tuggy.

He was trying all the time to think of powerful effects that would surprise the audience and make them clap.

There was, for instance, the "unearthly music" that was suddenly to be heard at one point in the masque when Nick waved his magic wand.

As it was supposed to come from invisible musicians, Mr. Tuggy decided that the real players must be hidden in a pit at one side of the stage, covered over with green netting and strewn with grass. The workmen grumbled but dug the great hole as he directed.

"It won't be 'unearthly music' if it comes out of the earth," Nick whispered to Celia.

"No—but it will have 'a powerful effect'," she giggled.

Mr. Tuggy scratched his head a long time, trying to think of another powerful effect for the final triumphant appearance of Apollo and Diana. If they just walked on in the midst of the fireworks and the Evil Spirits' howling, the audience would hardly notice them.

It was Nick who had the bright idea. At the end of the rehearsal, as the rest of the cast were trooping away across the park, he and Celia stayed to speak to the schoolmaster.

"Suppose, sir, we suddenly appeared over there?"

He pointed across to the boathouse. Mr. Tuggy looked doubtful.

"It is a long way, Nicholas. It will be getting dusk by then. Would the audience see you?"

But Nick had it all worked out in his mind.

"We could have a mighty blare of trumpets, sir—"

"Ye-es."

"And a great blaze of golden fireworks from behind the boathouse—gold because I'm the Sun God. Everyone would look that way and they'd see me in the light of them—"

"And me," Celia reminded him.

"A powerful effect, indeed," said Mr. Tuggy. "There is only one thing, Nicholas. You and your sister have still to reach the stage—it is a long way to come from the boathouse and you must be stately, you cannot run—"

"We should walk, sir—very stately."

"It will be too slow, it will spoil the ending."

"Not if we walk straight from the boat-house, sir—straight across the water."

"Across the water?"

Mr. Tuggy stared down at him as though he feared he had gone mad.

"On planks, sir. Just an inch or two

under the top of the water. The audience wouldn't see them."

"Explain yourself, boy!"

Nick grinned. "Do you remember the floods last winter, sir? How the lake rose two feet or more? It came right up over the landing-stage. And when the boatman walked out to the end—"

"I see," said Mr. Tuggy as light dawned. "You mean, he looked as though he were walking on the surface of the water?"

"Like Jesus in the Bible," exclaimed Celia.

Excitedly, Nick pointed out how easy it would be. The workmen could drive some thick posts into the mud and shallow water. A causeway of planks could be laid across them. The straight line from boat-house to acting area was not so long—not half the distance the actors had to travel when they walked round the curving shore. The reeds would help to hide the submerged timber from even the sharpest eyes in the audience.

"The workmen will grumble," said Mr. Tuggy.

"But they will do it," said Nick. "They had better do it early in the mornings," he added, "before anyone is about. This is something we simply *must* keep secret until the day."

"I can't wait to see their faces," said Celia, though inwardly she felt a little scared at the thought of what she would have to do. It would be no easy thing, that stately entrance, stepping along wet planks through an inch of cold water, knowing that one false step would tumble her, head over heels, into the deeper water on either side.

"They will be amazed," agreed Mr. Tuggy, "and Her Majesty will be vastly entertained."

Nick said slyly, "It should have a most powerful effect, sir."

CHAPTER THREE

THE days passed, the September sunshine bathed the land in warm gold, the preparations for the Queen's arrival went on at feverish speed.

Out of doors, the workmen banged and thumped and sawed as they made everything ready for the masque and the tournament. Within the house one heard snatches of music and song—and in all sorts of odd corners Nick and Celia could be found muttering their lines. The vast kitchen was full of delicious smells as the cooks produced mountains of saffron-cakes and gingerbread, venison pasties and cheese flans and quince pies and a host of other good things. The rest of the house, upstairs and down, was fragrant with perfume and herbs and sprinkled rose-water.

Mother flew hither and thither, ordering the servants, growing paler and more nervous day by day. Father limped from room to room, across the courtyard, round the gardens, bellowing like a good-natured bull as he urged the men forward with their tasks. Edward practised for the tournament, Margaret kept trying on different gowns and nagging Mother to lend her some jewels.

Down by the lake the children found it almost peaceful, though Mr. Tuggy worked them hard at rehearsals and made them try every movement again and again. Only their final walk across the water they dared not repeat, lest the secret get out and the "powerful effect" be spoiled. They did it once, when nobody was about, and were relieved to find that it was quite easy, though the water struck cold to their feet. The main thing was that the planks were firm and not slippery, and though people in the distance could not see them they were clearly visible to the children as they stepped out along them.

"It's only like walking through a puddle," said Nick.

"A very *long* puddle," said Celia with a shiver. She was thankful that her brother was supposed to lead her by the hand.

"You must mind how you set down your feet," Mr. Tuggy warned them. "Do not kick the water and make a splash. Remember, you are a god and goddess, not children paddling."

They promised to be as dignified as they could.

By the morning of the Queen's arrival even Mr. Tuggy was satisfied that everything was ready, though the masque would not be performed until the second evening.

All the boys and girls knew their lines and were well drilled in their exits and entrances. The musicians and singers were rehearsed in the dances and songs and fanfares of trumpets they were to provide.

The costumes had been made and fitted. Very glorious and fantastical they were. Nick wore a cloak and tunic of bright saffron, and a spiked crown to suggest the rays of the sun. Celia was to be clad in shining cloth-of-silver, her head-dress like a full moon. They no longer envied the Evil Spirits, who might have fearsome scowling masks but otherwise wore rather drab and bedraggled robes and had no poetry to say, and nothing much to do but gibber and yell. It was much finer to be Apollo and Diana.

Now all the costumes were safely stowed away in the tiring-room—the boathouse specially cleared for the purpose—along with the spears and shields and banners, the fireworks and all the other things.

Six gardeners in a row, with scythes sharp as razors, had worked their way across the acting area, shaving the grass until it was like smooth velvet.

In front, the Queen's pavilion stood up proudly, all crimson and gold, its curtains straining against the breeze. To one side lay the musicians' pit, hidden under netting and greenery.

The whole place had been made as tidy as the bedroom prepared for Her Majesty. Every dead leaf, every unwanted bough or swathe of cut grass, had been carried away to burn well out of sight beyond the boathouse.

If it had been possible to polish the surface of the lake like a mirror, Mr. Tuggy would certainly have asked for it to be done.

Everything was now right and ready. Even if it had not been, Mr. Tuggy could have done no more that morning. The Queen was coming. She had to be met at the market cross in the town three miles away, and they must all be there, and Mr.

Tuggy must make his speech of welcome.

It was a long procession on horseback that set out from Fairfield Hall to meet the Queen and escort her back.

Father rode in front, and with him all the chief gentlemen of the district, splendid in their plumed caps and flowing capes.

Nick and Celia came a long way behind, Nick in his best doublet and his plum-coloured jerkin laced over it, with clean starched ruff and not a wrinkle in his hose, bestriding his grey pony, Prince, while Celia perched side-saddle on Roan Barbary, looking quite a grand young lady in her long gown and kirtle.

"Mind you don't fall off," murmured Edward, reining in his horse as he moved up the column to his own place.

"I don't fall off," said Celia indignantly. She was a good rider and proud of it.

"One can fall off other things besides ponies," said her big brother. "One could

41

look very foolish in front of the Queen—and very wet." The two children looked at him aghast. "Remember," went on Edward mysteriously, "you are supposed to be Apollo and Diana tomorrow night—not Neptune and one of his mermaids. It would be sad if someone took away a few planks."

With a chuckle he rode on to join his friends nearer the front of the procession.

"He knows about the causeway," hissed Nick.

Celia's heart sank. " He wouldn't dare . . ." she faltered.

"It would be just like him," said Nick gloomily. "But, no, I don't think he would. He couldn't be such a beast."

All the same, he wondered.

Luckily the excitement of the Queen's arrival soon drove all thought of Edward and his tricks out of both their minds.

The cavalcade reached the town half an hour before the Queen. They all packed into the cobbled market square, the horse-men pressed closely, knee to knee, with just a space left for the royal coach to drive up to the stone cross.

The coach was splendid, glistening with gold and paint. It was drawn by six light grey horses. Celia gasped when she saw them, for their manes and tails were bright orange. Nick whispered that they were only dyed that colour. They were very special horses, bought from Hungary.

There were so many fine gentlemen in plumed hats, so many tall Yeomen of the Guard with flashing spears, that the child-ren had to crane their necks for a glimpse of Queen Elizabeth as she stepped from the coach. Yet it was a wonderful moment, worth waiting for, like the sun coming out. She was all they had expected, and more—proud and straight, yet sweetly smiling to left and right, brilliant as a peacock in her flowing gown all studded with pearls. The high ruff stood up behind her head like the peacock's tail, and there were more pearls in her red-gold hair.

"*Oh!*" said Celia softly, and she was not the only one in that vast crowd who gasped.

She understood now why Mr. Tuggy had called Her Majesty "Gloriana" in his verses, and compared her with the Fairy

Queen. And now Father—their own father—was bowing over that royal hand and kissing it in welcome.

Mr. Tuggy could be heard pattering out his Latin speech. Once he faltered, and the Queen's clear voice cut in quickly: "I thank you, Mr. Tuggy. You are a man of wit and wisdom. To speak briefly, and to the point, as you do, is a great gift." She turned away, and Mr. Tuggy's squeaky voice was heard no more.

"He had a lot more written out," said Nick. "He must have lost his place, and she thought he had finished."

It was as well, for the horses were eager to get moving again. There was a mighty cheer as the Queen stepped back into her coach. The crowd somehow unwound themselves into an orderly procession behind it. It was a much longer column now, because of all the courtiers and guards who had come with the Queen. Last of all followed the royal servants with dozens of rumbling two-wheeled carts, piled up with mountains of baggage.

It was a day that no one at Fairfield Hall was likely to forget.

By the time Nick and Celia reached home the front of the column had already dispersed. Mother had welcomed the Queen with a curtsey and taken her indoors. The coach had rumbled away and the gentlemen were standing about with goblets of wine and the servants were leading the horses to the stable-yard.

The children slipped from their saddles, handed over their ponies to a groom, and hurried inside to catch what glimpses they could of Her Majesty.

Glimpses were about as much as they got.

It was strange to find their own home— the great house they had known since babyhood—transformed for two days into a royal residence. Unfamiliar faces met them at every turn. Grand courtiers chatted in corners with elegant maids of honour. Sentries stood by the broad staircase leading up to the Queen's apartments, sturdy men in scarlet uniforms with the golden rose of the Tudors. Even Nick and Celia were told they must not try to pass the Yeomen of the Guard—it felt odd being forbidden to use the main stairs in their own home, but it did not matter since their own bedrooms were in the east wing and were reached by another staircase.

"Father need not have worried," said Celia. "I don't see how anyone could get near the Queen to harm her."

Mother had told them how it had been no use to make up Her Majesty's bed before she arrived because only the Yeomen of the Guard were allowed to touch it. It was their duty to examine each sheet and coverlet separately before laying it on the bed and tucking it in.

It was the same with the Queen's dinner, to make sure that nobody tried to poison hcr. Nick and Celia squeezed into a high gallery looking down into the banquet-hall and watched the ceremony of serving Her Majesty's meal.

Officers laid the table, kneeling as they spread the cloth and set out the silver salt-cellar and the bread. Then two dozen Yeomen filed in, each bearing a golden dish of food. A lady-in-waiting came forward with a knife, cut a little piece from each delicacy, and gave it to the Yeoman carrying it, to eat.

The children held their breath. What if—somehow—one of the dishes *had* been poisoned? But all was well. Each man seemed to enjoy his taste. No one collapsed on the floor in agony.

Now the trumpets sounded. And the Queen and her ladies sailed in—there was no other word for it, because in their full-spread rustling skirts they came down the hall like a fleet of ships. The Queen had changed her dress and was a figure of splendour in flame-coloured silk. And their mother fluttered just behind her, elegant in blue and silver.

Nick and Celia peered down from the balcony, eager to miss nothing. They noticed that the Queen chose simple food herself, and drank only a little ale, but the courtiers feasted happily on the rich banquet prepared for them. The Queen smiled and joked with those near to her, but everybody was very respectful. It was a wonderful thing, thought Celia, to be such a grand lady, the grandest lady in all the world, and yet be so natural, not stiff or proud. Feared by her enemies, loved by her people—that was the great Elizabeth.

When the tables had been cleared away there was dancing, and the Queen was as lively as anyone. Fast dances and slow dances, she tried them all—Shake-a-Trot, the Bishop of Chester's Jig, Lady Carey's Dump, and Dusty-My-Dear. Even when she sat down for a short rest they could see her foot tapping, her hand waving in time to the music.

The children watched, fascinated. They

would remember this for the rest of their lives, this evening when the Queen of England danced in their own house. They did not notice the passing of time until Mother leant over their shoulders, whispering. She had not forgotten them amid all the anxieties of that busy day.

"Bed," she ordered. "Remember the masque tomorrow."

They did not dare to argue. They went off to the little bedrooms they occupied, next to each other, in the east wing, far from the music and laughter in the hall.

"I shall never get to sleep," said Nick.

But he did. The next thing he knew was that Celia was shaking him. She had pulled aside his bed-curtains and she stood there in a shaft of bright moonlight slanting through the window.

"Nick," she said, "there's someone down by the lake. I think it's Edward—he's going to play a trick on us!"

CHAPTER FOUR

HER words roused Nick like a pail of cold water thrown over him. He leapt from his bed and pattered to the window.

Edward's mocking words rushed back into his mind. "It would be sad if someone took away a few planks . . ."

"Look," said Celia.

It was a night of cloud patches, scudding across the heavens before a light easterly wind. The full moon would show for a few moments, bathing the park and lake in silver. Then it would vanish, leaving dark gloom, until just as suddenly it flashed out again like a watchman's lantern. Very soon, in any case, it would go down behind the wooded hills.

"Yes," said Nick. Even at that distance his keen eyes spotted a figure at the

water's edge. He clenched his fists with fury. Edward was a brute. What could one do with big brothers like that? He raged with the helplessness that only small boys and girls know when they have to battle against the strong and the unkind.

Yet, he thought, why be helpless? He began to pull on his clothes.

"Nick! You're not going down there— at this time of night?"

"Why not?" he grunted, muffled by his shirt. "If we can get there before he's finished we can make him put the planks back. He won't *dare* not to, once he knows we've seen him. If he didn't, and we told Father, he'd get such a flogging, big as he is. Father would stop him riding in the tournament—"

"I'm coming with you." She scuttled through the door into her own room.

"I shan't wait," he called after her. "It's no use if we don't catch him at it."

Celia dressed more quickly than she

ever had in her life before, and as he tip-
toed down the stairway, a pale figure in
the fitful moonlight which chose that
moment to pour through the great
window, she was creeping close behind.

It was lucky now that they were a long way from the bedchambers of the Queen and her ladies, for there were no sentries in this wing of the house. No one stirred, no one cried out when they made a loose board creak, no one heard the click as they opened a casement, climbed over the windowsill, and dropped softly on to the paved terrace below.

Outside, there was more risk than they had realized. As they reached the steps leading down into the garden they heard the slow, heavy tread of a man walking along the terrace behind them. They had just time to slip down the steps and crouch among the bushes before the sinking moon came from behind the clouds and once more lit up the whole scene with the brightness of day.

The footfalls stopped. They heard the thud as the sentry brought down the butt of his halberd on the paving and stood there, scanning the garden below with its network of paths and little flowerbeds, its rows of yews clipped into the shapes of birds and animals.

One tree was most cunningly trained

into the likeness of a peacock. The children crouched behind its spread tail, almost afraid to draw their breath, until the sentry shouldered his halberd and continued his patrol. Then, as the moon went behind another cloud, darkness swept the garden like a black flood. They seized their chance and raced silently for the arched gate in the wall.

As they gained the safety of the park, the moon peeped out once more. But it hung low in the sky now, touching the treetops beyond the lake. Again the ragged clouds streamed across the silver circle. When they had passed, the moon had sunk behind the wooded ridge. Nick knew it would be darker than ever now for the next hour, until the day began to break.

Still, they could just see where they were going, and it was all familiar ground.

Long, low bands of mist rose from the lake in front, glimmering and ghostly pale against the blackness of the night.

Not all of it was mist. The children sniffed wood-smoke. Some of the greyness came from the smouldering bonfires on the far side of the boathouse.

Once, for a moment, they had a shock. As they drew near the boathouse it was as though a bright red eye, like a dragon's, glowed fiercely in front of them. Celia stifled a gasp, but Nick gripped her arm.

"Silly!" he hissed. "It's only the fire."

A puff of wind across the water had fanned the ashes. As the breeze fell again, the dragon's eye faded and a stronger whiff of burning leaves and branches came to their nostrils.

Mist and smoke were equally useful to hide their stealthy approach in case Edward should look up from his work.

They could hear him plainly now. Evidently he had brought a friend to help him. The children caught low voices and the hollow rumble and thud of heavy wooden objects being dragged about.

Nick and Celia had made for the boathouse itself. It was the easiest place to find in that gloom. Also, it gave them cover.

Nick's heart was beating madly, and it was not only due to their breathless race across the park.

Edward would not be pleased when they jumped out upon him and showed that his mean trick was not going to work. In fact he would be furious, especially as he had someone with him. No one liked his friends to see him beaten by his small brother and sister.

Nick's courage nearly failed him. He was tempted not to show himself and challenge Edward after all. Suppose he and Celia just crept back to the house now, and left the whole business until the morning?

Surely, if they warned Mr. Tuggy and he went down for himself and saw that the causeway had been tampered with, he could get hold of the workmen again and have it put right before the performance?

Nick bit his lip. It was a cowardly way out. It would make much more trouble in the end.

The poor workmen would be as furious as Edward if they had to carry out the repairs when they should have been watching the tournament. Also, they would have to work in broad daylight, and everybody would know about the hidden causeway, and the surprise would be spoilt at the end of the masque.

Father would learn what Edward had done. Nick did not like to imagine what Father would say to Edward. He knew very well what Father would say to his younger son.

He would want to know why Nick had not been brave enough to speak out before the damage was done. If you were there, he would say, why on earth didn't you stop him? He'd have put everything right again before dawn, and no one would have been the wiser!

Father would think Nick a silly little fool and a coward. Nick decided he would rather face an angry brother than a scornful father.

These thoughts raced through his mind in the few moments they spent crouched behind the boathouse, regaining their breath.

Suddenly Celia whispered in a scared voice: "What if it isn't Edward at all?"

CHAPTER FIVE

"WHO else could it be?" he retorted
crossly. Annoyed with himself for
his own fears, he took it out on his sister
unfairly.

He could guess that she had been think-
ing in the same way. Now she wanted an
excuse to give up and do nothing. Well,
they were not going to. They were not
going to scuttle back to their beds like a
pair of terrified mice.

There was a story told of Father in his
young days when he fought for the Queen
and got the leg-wound that had made
him limp ever afterwards. He had come
upon a Spanish outpost in the woods. He
had only two soldiers with him, but there
was no time to get help. So they attacked
the Spaniards, although there were twenty
of them, and the Spaniards had run away

in terror. People called Father a hero, but Father just said he had done the only possible thing.

Surely they could be as bold as that? In their own park? When it was only against their own brother?

But was it?

Nick had a sudden doubt as he peered round the corner of the boathouse.

It was not too dark to see two shadowy figures moving about, but he was not sure that either of them was Edward. They spoke seldom, and in such low voices that he could not recognize them from their speech.

One thing was certainly puzzling. They were not doing anything to the causeway. They were not even near the edge of the lake. They were on the far side of the grassy stage, close to the pavilion from which the Queen was to watch the performance.

"What are they moving?" Celia asked.

He strained his eyes to peer through the gloom. It sounded almost as though they were trundling a little barrel across the lawn.

"It's thieves," Celia insisted.

"Thieves?" he echoed scornfully. Celia fancied things. All the fine costumes were safe in the boathouse. "What is there to steal over there?"

"I-I don't know," she faltered. He felt sure now that it was her fear of Edward. She had thought of this wild idea of thieves as the excuse she needed to go running back to the house.

"Perhaps," she added faintly, "it's the ale that was brought down ready for the musicians."

"Don't be stupid. If they were going to steal the ale they wouldn't be hiding it under the Queen's pavilion."

"Is that what they're doing?"

"Looks like it." Nick scowled at the two grey shapes across the gap of glimmering water. "Some trick of Edward's. Surely he wouldn't dare to meddle with the place where *she's* going to sit—"

"I don't like it, Nick."

"We must stop him, then." He tried to sound bold and masterful. He was afraid his sister was on the verge of panic.

Suddenly one of his bright ideas came to him. He crept back to the boathouse door, stooped for the key that was kept hidden under a stone, and slid it into the lock.

"What are you going to do?"

"Give them the fright of their lives."

Once inside the boathouse he was able to raise his voice slightly. He spoke rapidly, making her obey.

"Put this on your head. Careful!" He handed her one of the weird head-coverings made for the Evil Spirits in the play. There was no difficulty about finding them in the darkness. Because of their awkward branching horns they could not be piled up among the other costumes. They were stuck on wooden pegs high on the wall.

"Don't argue," he went on. He seized another head-dress for himself and pulled it down over his ears. He had tried these things on at rehearsal, never dreaming that the chance to wear one would ever come. "This will scare even Edward," he said, and Celia answered with a giggling "Yes" though her voice was muffled under the hideous disguise.

"If only we had a lighted taper," said Nick, "we could throw fire-crackers at them. That would be just the finishing touch."

"But we *have*." Celia sounded much braver now. It was as though covering her face had lent her courage.

"Have what?"

"The bonfire."

"Of course! I can get a burning twig."

"I will. You know where the fireworks were put."

She sped across to the nearest of the smouldering rubbish-heaps. By the time she was back, a red-tipped branch glowing in her hand, Nick had taken half a dozen jumping crackers out of the box and stuffed them carefully inside his doublet.

"Can *I* have some?" she whispered as he took the branch and held the hot end well away from him.

"No." He knew it was Father's strict rule. Celia was too young to handle fireworks. "But when I let them off," he promised hoarsely, "you can yell and scream as much as you like. So they take us for devils."

It seemed a lifetime since Celia had wakened him from sleep. Yet there was still no glimmer of dawn in the eastern sky. The whole adventure—the escape from the silent house, the race across the misty park, the hasty whisperings at the boathouse—could not have taken more than half an hour.

There was not a moment more to be lost, though, or Edward and his friend would finish whatever they were doing and be gone.

"Come on," said Nick between his teeth. "Along the causeway."

He stepped out along the planks. He could just see them dimly in front of his feet. The water struck icy cold through his shoes and he had to bite his lip to hold

back a gasp. He dared not look round, but he knew Celia was close behind. He could not give her his hand as he did in the play. He needed both hands for the fireworks and the smouldering twig.

He would take ten steps, then set off the first of the jumping crackers. If he waited longer, Edward might glance up and see the ruby glint of light.

Five, six . . .

He heard one of the shadowy figures speak. It was not Edward's voice.

Seven, eight . . .

Edward answered. Only—that did not sound like Edward's voice either. Nick caught only the tail-end of the words. Perhaps it was, "I refuse". Only the last bit—"fuse"—came distinctly across the water.

Nick stopped short. Celia almost bumped into him from behind. Neither of those figures was their brother. Who were they then? Had Celia been right after all?

"Go on," she urged him. She had noticed nothing strange.

A wild kind of despair seized Nick. He no longer knew what was going on, but he could bear no more hesitations. They had come too far to turn back now.

He took a deep breath and puffed the end of his twig until the fire glowed. Then he lit the first of his jumping crackers and hurled it through the air.

Celia let out a terrifying screech behind him. He lit the second firework and stalked forward, uttering fearsome yells.

Celia told him afterwards how frightening he had looked in the flicker and flash of the crackers, with that towering headdress and the branching horns.

It must have been far more alarming for the two men, taken completely by surprise, as they turned to see two such spectres advancing upon them—and apparently walking on the surface of the lake.

"*Yaaa-ah!*" howled Nick.

He threw the last of his fireworks and began to run the last few yards along the causeway, waving his arms and crooking his fingers in a diabolical manner.

The fireworks leapt and spat and bounced across the grass, showering sparks as far as the pavilion and lighting up the whole scene. He saw the two men's startled faces—faces completely unknown to him. Then they turned and fled.

The plan had succeeded. Nick was so relieved that he let out a final yell of fiendish triumph.

And then suddenly there was a blinding flash, a terrific explosion, as the whole pavilion unfolded against the sky like a flower of flame.

To the children it felt as though a giant's hot hand had flipped them, knocking them off the causeway into the chilly waters of the lake. Overhead, it rained fire. Blazing fragments sizzled as they fell.

CHAPTER SIX

" ARE you all right?" Nick managed
to gasp.

"I-I think s-so," Celia answered with
chattering teeth. Both their masks had been
blown off by the blast of the explosion.

The water was quite shallow but very
cold. The mud sucked at their feet, but
they managed to flounder back to the
landing-stage and haul themselves on to
it like stranded fish. Then they crawled
the last few yards to the shore.

There was a foul stench of gunpowder
in the air, more than a thousand fireworks
would have made. There was the smell of
scorched cloth and painted wood also.
Raising his head cautiously, Nick could
not make out what had happened to the
Queen's pavilion.

That tremendous bang had woken the

78

whole world, it seemed. The night was suddenly full of twittering voices—small, at first, in the distance like birds, then louder and deeper as they grew nearer.

All the way down from the great house the sloping park was alive with dancing torches. Their red light glinted on steel points and blades.

Mr. Tuggy's open-air theatre filled with Yeomen of the Guard, scurrying and poking about like a pack of hounds. Some of the Fairfield servants came with them. As Nick and Celia went shakily forward they came face to face with their astonished brother. Edward had obviously risen straight from his bed, for his shirt was half out of his hose and he wore no doublet.

Before they could answer his startled questions the Yeomen of the Guard called out that they had found a strange man, stunned and powder-singed, collapsed upon the grass. A second man was heard groaning close by. In running away he had fallen straight into the hidden pit dug for the musicians, and had broken his leg. He too was seized by the guard and carried off.

Halfway back to the house, the children met Father, limping along at a surprising speed, a bare sword in his hand. He stared at them amazed. "Are you all right?" he asked. "Good. You will have to explain yourselves later. I must see what is happening down there. Back to the house with you!" Within half an hour, as dawn began to brighten the sky outside the tall windows, they sat sipping hot drinks in the parlour and telling him their story.

"A fine thing to happen at our house," he said with a groan. "Those scoundrels meant to kill the Queen." He stretched out his arms and put a hand round each of the children. "Thank God you were wakeful and went down there—and thank God you took no harm yourselves." He stood up. "Back to your beds now, and try to sleep. You will have to answer more questions later, but have no fear. Just speak the truth."

There was not much hope that the

children would sleep after that. Nick sat on the edge of Celia's bed and they talked in low voices—excitedly about what had happened, and rather dismally about what would happen next. Would the masque be played? Or would the Queen get into her coach as soon as she learned of the plot to blow her up with gunpowder, and drive away from Fairfield Hall for ever?

But that, they soon found, was not the way with royal visits. The programme sailed grandly on exactly as planned, and as if nothing had happened. During the tournament they slipped away and went down to the lake. The Queen's pavilion had been rebuilt with magical speed—fresh boards and corner-posts and rails and curtains being rushed to the spot and put together during the morning. No one could see where the plotter had tumbled into the musicians' pit.

Everybody knew by now about the explosion and the wicked plan to kill Her Majesty, but the details of what exactly had happened were still secret. Few people had heard yet that the children had been involved, and even those few had no idea that there was a causeway under the water

which had played a vital part in exposing the plot.

Mr. Tuggy smiled as he checked every detail for the last time. "Everything is right, everything is ready," he said. "And our own little secret is still quite safe."

It was a warm September evening, sweet and mellow as a pear. The sun went down in glory behind the woods, turning the lake into a mirror of gold, and the Queen in *her* glory came down through the park,

attended by all her fine ladies and gentle-men, and took her seat to watch the enter-tainment.

The trumpets blew, the masque began. In clear voices, like bells, the boys and girls recited their lines. Nick and Celia spoke up with the rest. All memory of the night's perilous adventure was thrust out of their minds. They were acting under the eyes of their mighty sovereign. She was sitting there, a resplendent figure under the canopy, her dress a shimmer of countless pearls. Nothing mattered but to remember their words and play their parts as Mr. Tuggy had taught them.

The sunset faded from the sky. Now the torches flared, reflected in the reedy shal-lows. The music from underground took all the audience by surprise. Nick could see the Queen clapping her ringed hands in approval. The Evil Spirits delighted everyone with their frightful noises and caperings. But it was the grand climax that people still talked about for years afterwards—the climax when Apollo came to the rescue in a shower of golden rain, stepping across the surface of the lake, hand in hand with his goddess sister, and put the Evil Spirits to flight.

The Queen laughed and applauded as long as anyone. And when the children went forward across the grass to speak their closing lines, Nick making his grandest bow and Celia her lowest curtsey, the Queen stretched out her hands and took theirs, and drew them up on to the carpeted platform beside her. They stood there, dazed with happiness, not knowing if they ought to kneel before her magnificence, and then suddenly she made them feel almost at home, her voice was so kindly, her eyes twinkling with so much fun.

Mr. Tuggy was standing modestly in the background. She beckoned him and he advanced, bowing and blushing.

"You have done well, Mr. Tuggy, you and all your young players. I thank you heartily." Then, in a lower tone, she added: "But if I am not mistaken these two deserve more special thanks." She smiled down at the children and said: "You shall both take supper with me tonight. I think you have more to tell me than Mr. Tuggy wrote out for you in his pretty verses."

Nick gulped and tried to answer, "Yes, Your Majesty," but his lips produced no sound.

It had been a long, wonderful day—and the best was yet to come.

THE END